BERTIE
WINGS IT!

by

LESLIE GORIN

illustrated by

BRENDAN KEARNEY

STERLING CHILDREN'S BOOKS
New York

Bertie peered out from his nest and knew it was time.

His home felt small now that he was big.
The sky didn't seem so scary. And today,
the sun smiled and the breeze beckoned
as never before.

"Yes!" said Bertie.
"Today is the day that I fly!"

He stepped from the edge of his nest. His wings tingled with excitement.

"Ready . . . set . . ."

A booming voice knocked Bertie backward.

"Admiral Bird here. Ten-hut—listen up! You want to fly? Well, you can't just wing it. You need skills! Drills! Admiral Bird's School of Fly Higher Education has it all. Come enlist—I insist!"

Bertie thought flying was what birdies did naturally.
But Admiral Bird was a very persuasive penguin, so
Bertie skittered down and signed up.

During class, Bertie listened to lectures. He watched films. He read maps, learned apps, and ran laps.

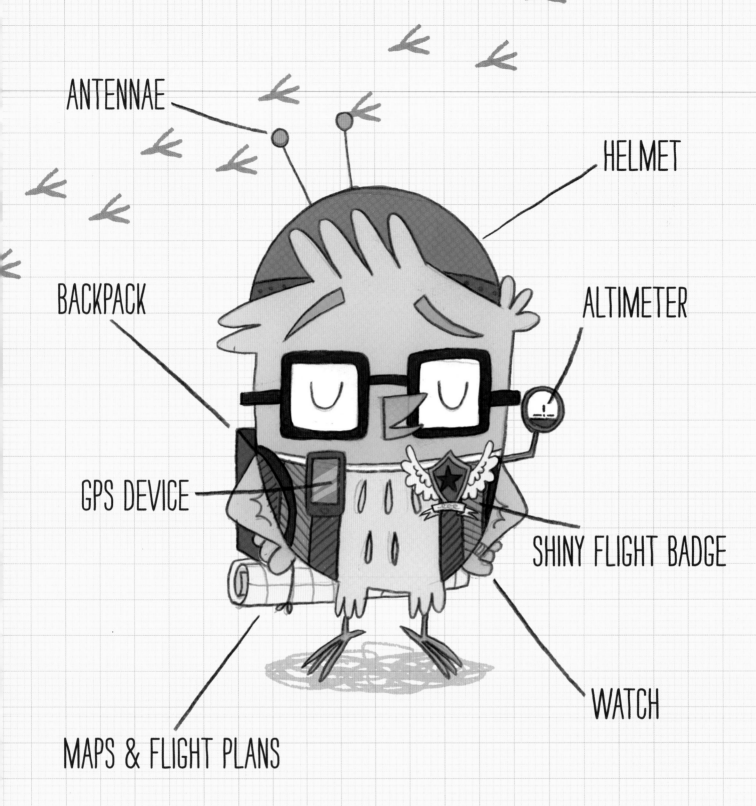

ANTENNAE

HELMET

BACKPACK

ALTIMETER

GPS DEVICE

SHINY FLIGHT BADGE

WATCH

MAPS & FLIGHT PLANS

He got gizmos and gadgets up the gazoo, and a
shiny flight badge, too. Soon he knew all about flying . . .
but he never actually flew.
Even so, he was gung ho to give it a go.

He lugged his new tools up his tree and stepped from the edge of his nest. **"Ready . . . set . . ."**

"NO!"

A screeching voice knocked Bertie sideways.

"Prunella Flapdoodle here. You can't fly without proper papers! You need a license. Permit. Engine checks. Emissions tests. Can't have you stinking up the skies, you know. Take a number. We'll call when it's your turn."

Papers? No one had said anything about papers. But Prunella was not an emu to pooh-pooh, so Bertie went to the back of the crowd.

Hours later, Bertie had headlights, hoses,
brakes, belts, and papers that reached the sky . . .

. . . but he still hadn't tried to fly.

Bertie waddled home, hoping by now he was set to soar.

He dragged his baggage up his tree and stepped to the edge of his nest.

"Ready . . . set . . ."

"NO!"

A squawking voice knocked Bertie cockeyed.

"Monique von Beaque here. Dahling, whatever are you thinking, making your debut dressed like a dodo? You need Monique von Beaque's Chic Bird-tique! Trust me, dahling—you'll fly higher in my attire!"

Bertie never knew he needed high fashion to fly. But Monique was a very convincing kiwi, so Bertie trundled down and gussied up.

Monique von Beaqué's
CHIC BIRD-TIQUE

Bertie was one dapper flapper . . .

He got hipster pants

and furs from France

frou-frou frocks and
spiffy socks

a ruby ring and
birdie bling.

But he still hadn't flown.
Bertie staggered home, aching
to sail the skies.

He huffed and puffed up his tree and
stepped to the edge of the branch.

"Ready . . . set . . .

Poor Bertie! His gear was in pieces. His gizmos were no-goes. So were his cool clothes. How could he fly without those?

"It's useless," moaned Bertie. "I'm grounded for life!"
Bertie's eyes filled with tears. He covered his face with his wings.
But then, Bertie noticed something.

Without all his . . .

MAPS

FROCKS

APPS

CHARTS

SOCKS

PARTS

AND PAPERS

. . . he felt lighter.
Freer.

And deep down inside, he knew that he knew—he had *always* known—how to fly.

He raced up his tree. His heart fluttered with joy.

"Ready . . . set . . .